Paddington
and the
Christmas Surprise

First published in hardback by HarperCollins Publishers, USA, in 1997
First published in hardback in Great Britain by Collins in 1997
First published in paperback by Picture Lions in 1998
New edition published in paperback by HarperCollins Children's Books in 2008
This edition published in 2014

5 7 9 10 8 6 4

ISBN: 978-0-00-725773-7

Collins and Picture Lions are imprints of HarperCollins Publishers Ltd.
HarperCollins Children's Books is a division of HarperCollins Publishers Ltd.

Text copyright © Michael Bond 1997, 2008
Illustrations copyright © R. W. Alley 1997, 2008

Visit our website at: www.harpercollins.co.uk

Printed in China

Michael Bond
Paddington
and the
Christmas Surprise

Illustrated by R. W. Alley

HarperCollins *Children's Books*

One Christmas Paddington announced he was taking the Brown family to Barkridges store to see Santa Claus.

"It's very good value," he explained. "Apart from meeting Mr Claus, there's a sleigh ride through Winter Wonderland and you get to visit his workshop at the North Pole. We might even see where he makes his marmalade."

"I doubt if Santa makes his own marmalade," said Mrs Brown nervously, as Paddington led the way on to the escalator.

"It would make all the presents sticky," agreed Jonathan.

"Not to mention his beard," added Judy. "Besides, he's much too busy."

"That's more than you can say for Barkridges," remarked Mr Brown gloomily, as he brought up the rear. "There's hardly anyone here."

There were two signs at the top of the escalator, one pointing
to Santa Claus, and one pointing to Winter Wonderland.

"I think I may visit Santa Claus first," announced
Paddington, "in case the sleigh gets stuck in the snow."

He got down on his paws and knees in order to get
a better look and make sure it wasn't too deep.

Just then he looked up and saw a man staring down at him.

"Are you a boy or a girl?" asked the store manager.

"I'm neither," said Paddington. "I'm a bear."

"You look more like a large creepy-crawly to me," said the man distastefully.

"Perhaps you had better come back next year when you've made up your mind."

"Come back next year," repeated Paddington hotly. "But I've brought my Christmas list. I thought it would save the postage."

The Browns were too far away
to hear what was being said but
from the look on Paddington's
face they guessed something
must be wrong.

"Hurry up," called Mrs Bird.
"We're all ready to go."

"Oh dear, Henry," said Mrs Brown.
"I do hope the sleigh ride is a success.
Paddington's been saving his bun
money for ages and he'll be
most upset if it doesn't live
up to his expectations."

As Paddington clambered aboard
and they set off, Mr Brown held
up a leaflet.

"Listen everybody," he called.
"First of all, we go past Santa's
winter garden."

"I think I prefer Mrs Bird's
window box," said Paddington.

The Browns exchanged anxious
glances. It didn't seem a very good
start to the outing.

"How about this one, then?" continued Mr Brown, as they turned a corner. "It's the stable where Santa keeps his reindeer."

Paddington didn't say anything. From where he was sitting it looked more like a dog kennel and the only reindeer he could see was a plastic one that had fallen over in the snow.

The North Pole.

Next, Mr Brown pointed to a very tall tower with a flashing light at the top.

"That's the lighthouse at the North Pole," he said. "It's there to make sure Santa arrives back home safe and sound after he's delivered all his presents."

Paddington gave it a hard stare. "I think there must be a wire loose, Mr Brown," he exclaimed. "The light keeps going on and off."

"Lighthouses are supposed to flash," broke in Jonathan. "They all send out a different signal so that people know exactly where they are."

But Paddington wasn't listening. He was counting the number of buns it had taken to pay for the outing.

"Now, this might be more interesting." Mr Brown tried
to strike a cheerful note as they drew nearer to a big house
with mechanical figures moving behind every window.
"We're about to enter Santa's workshop."

"Look at the elves," called Judy.

She turned round in order to explain elves to Paddington,
but as she did so she gave a cry of alarm, for he was
nowhere to be seen.

"Do something, Henry!" cried Mrs Brown when she saw what had happened.

"Do something?" repeated Mr Brown. "What can I do from inside the middle of a workshop?"

"We haven't reached the end of the tour," warned Mrs Bird. "Paddington will be most upset if he misses any of it."

Mr Brown tried to put a brave face on things, but when
they reached the end of the ride and there was still no
sign of Paddington, he looked as worried as any of them.

He called to one of Santa's helpers.

"There's a bear fallen into our works?" repeated the man.
"I'll send for the manager at once!"

"Bear?" exclaimed the manager. "Did I hear someone say bear? If it's the one I met earlier, I'm not surprised he's missing. A troublemaker if ever I saw one. Blue duffle coat... old hat. I'd recognise him anywhere. Leave it to me – I'll find him."

"We're certainly not going until you have," warned Mrs Bird. "And what's more, if I know that bear he'll be wanting his money back."

"No one has ever asked for their money back before," wailed the manager.

"There's a first time for everything," said Mrs Bird grimly.

As the manager disappeared
through one door, Paddington
came through another.

"I think I've found the fault
in the lighthouse, Mr Brown,"
he called. "Bears are good
at mending things and…"

But before he had a
chance to finish there was
a loud bang from somewhere
inside Santa's workshop,
and all the lights went out.

"Where is he?" shouted the manager. "Where is he?
I'll give him a present he won't forget in a hurry!"

Mrs Bird took a firm grip of her umbrella.

"Come along, everyone," she called.

"I think we've had enough wonders for one day."

"Paddington's certainly hit the headlines," said Mr Brown at breakfast the next morning. "Listen to this: 'Strange Goings-on in London Store'."

"One thing's certain," said Mrs Brown. "We shan't be allowed into Barkridges again in a hurry."

"I don't know," broke in Jonathan. "Listen to this one: 'Crowds Flock to Santa's Workshop. Search for Mystery Bear Goes On'."

Everyone was so busy reading the newspapers that they didn't notice Mrs Bird leave the room. She had an important telephone call to make.

"Barkridges," said the manager, several days later, "wishes you all a very Merry Christmas. Ever since this young bear first honoured us with a visit we've had queues outside our store. It's quite like old times."

He turned to Mrs Bird. "And thank you, dear lady, for telephoning us when you did."

"Perhaps I could do some more repairs for you?" said Paddington hopefully.

"I don't think that will be necessary," said the manager hastily. "Besides, Santa is waiting to see you. After you've all had a free sleigh ride."

It was a merry party of Browns who set off on their journey through Winter Wonderland. This time everything worked perfectly, and when they came to the end of the ride Santa Claus was waiting to greet them.

"Ho ho ho,"

he boomed.
"And who have we here?"
"I'm a bear, Mr Claus," said Paddington. "And I come from Darkest Peru."

"Well," said Santa, reaching behind his chair, "in that case I think I know just what you would like."

Paddington nearly fell over backwards with surprise as Santa Claus held up an enormous jar. There was a label on the side that said **HOME-MADE** and it was tied at the top with a big red bow.

"It's my favourite, Mr Claus!" he cried. "How did you guess?"

Mrs Bird's face went pink as Santa gave her a knowing smile.

"One of the nicest things about Santa Claus," she said
hastily, "is that he knows exactly what everyone wants
for Christmas. That's what makes him so special."

"And he makes his own marmalade," said Paddington happily.
"I knew he would!"